Tommy Franks

Desperate and Lonely Housewives, a Novel

Beautiful and Sexy Women of Waterford

To order additional copies, please contact us.
BookSurge
www.booksurge.com
1-866-308-6235
orders@booksurge.com

DEDICATION

I dedicate this incredible and sexy book to my lovely and beautiful wife (Karen Lovejoy Harrison Franks) who believes in me and encourages me in my daily life.

.

CONTENTS

INTRODUCTION

This fictional book **Desperate and Lonely Housewives, a Novel: Beautiful and Sexy Women of Waterford** is about Hot, Sexy, Desperate, and Lonely Housewives who are aggressive and lonely in a small Southern town in which we call "Waterford" (fictional name). You will never read a more tantalizing and "give me more" sexy book. If you like this book, there may be a sequel. However, remember this book is purely "fictional"; so please do not associate any of the names, places, people, or even the book cover as reality.

Please do not speculate about any similarities of realism that you may have experienced or seen. These astonishing incidents and situations are filled with sex, humor, passion, love, intrigue, lies, deceit, promiscuity, and murder. Many of these events may seem real to you. If any of these stories are true, the names have been changed to protect the guilty. These incidents describe some of our current society's precarious morals, unsteady values, perilous sins, and hot passionate desires. Some of the fictional characters in these stories are individuals who have had difficulties in dealing with their own sexuality, loneliness, and identity. In short, sometimes their various temptations get the best of them. At times, it will seem as if almost every adult in Waterford is committed to some type of sexual temptation, desperation, or dependency…either mentally or physically.

Are these passionate fictional individuals an evil group of people? No! Are they human? Yes! That is why I am writing this book. I was born and reared in a small Southern town...so I pretty well know the lay of the land. I know the people, their idiosyncrasies, and southern mannerisms. For the most part, Southerners are heart warming, honest, patriotic and loyal Americans...loving, and hard working people; however, as we all know...sometimes, things get out of hand, even in small towns.

Waterford (USA) is a fictional atypical Southern town with high energy, beautiful, sexy, bored housewives who want to be treated with respect, dignity, passion, and romance.

If you are human, read this book. If you like humor and intrigue, read this book. If you are bored, read this book. If you want to have some fun, read this book. If you are a self-righteous individual, you may have difficulties and problems reading this book...or you may decide to venture out and have some imaginary fun, which would probably...do you a lot of good. Sit back and enjoy the read.

From the beginning of Biblical times (Genesis 6), man/woman has had desires that have led to tons of trouble within our society. Sodom and Gomorrah had trouble when the men of the city attempted to have sexual intercourse with two angels. Lot impregnated his own two daughters. Sex was very much a part of their lives.

Leah bargained with Rachel over an aphrodisiac (mandrakes) that her oldest son Reuben had found in the field (Genesis 30). In exchange for the aphrodisiac, Leah got to sleep and have sex all night with Jacob. The Bible does not say what Rachel did with the aphrodisiacs...but many believe she used them to make love and have sex with Jacob. Later, she did have two of his sons.

Another time in this same book (Genesis 34), Shechem, a young prince, raped Dinah, the daughter of Jacob and Leah. Afterwards, Dinah's brothers, Simeon and Levi went into the city of the rapist and killed him along with all the males to include the father of the criminal.

After the death of his wife, Judah, one of the twelve sons of Israel, decided that he wanted the services (sex) of a harlot (prostitute) (Genesis 38). They negotiated the terms. He slept with her, had sex, and she became pregnant with his child. However, he did not know that she was Tamar (his daughter-in-law). Therefore, in about three months he learned that his daughter-in-law had played the harlot and was now pregnant. She had been with a man.

Judah said, "Bring her here. We will burn her with fire until she is dead. We will teach her better than to be a prostitute and a disgrace."

As they were bringing her out for her execution, she said, "I am pregnant by the man who owns this seal, cord, and staff. Do any of you recognize them?"

Then suddenly, Judah knew that he was in fact the father of the child. He said, "Let her go for she is more righteous than I. I am the father. I have been a bad and naughty boy."

Later, she had twins.

As children, we learned the story of David and Bathsheba (2 Samuel 11). David was the king of the entire country. He was married. He was supposed to be out fighting a war; but instead, he was laying up in bed fantasizing about another man's wife. Finally, his passion and fantasies could take it no longer; therefore, he sent for her and committed sexual adultery with her immediately. She became pregnant with his child. David eventually had Bathsheba's husband murdered. Did he repent? Not then, but later, he came clean.

Even though the Law of Moses stated that incest was forbidden, it still happened in Biblical times. The Law said, "Cursed is he who has sex with his sister...the daughter of his father, or the daughter of his mother." Read on...

Perhaps, the most publicized example of incest centered around Amnon, the son of David. Amnon raped Tamar...his own sister (half sister). She had prepared a meal for him. When she brought the food to him, Amnon grabbed her and said, "Come to bed with me and have sex with me...my sister."

She said, "No, Amnon, do not do this awful deed. My brother, do not force me to do such a thing because this type of thing is wicked and should not be done in all of Israel. If you persist and do this thing, you will be known as a wicked fool."

But Amnon refused to listen. He raped her anyway!

This tragedy led to another tragedy. Tamar was also the sister of Absalom...another son of David. Absalom wanted revenge. He waited two long years and then evened the score with Amnon...who was also his half brother. He and his men killed Amnon at a sheepshearers' party.

Today, within our society, we have all kinds of prostitution. Even though this book is fictional, you will think that you are reading today's newspaper or watching the local news from your living room...about your local town. What is "prostitution"? In the Hebrew, it means to commit fornication or adultery, play the harlot or whore. In the Greek, it means idolater, harlot, or whore. In today's language, it means an individual who sells his/her body for the purpose of sexual intercourse. The price tag may not always be paid in dollars. It may be paid in special favors or power, especially in Washington D.C.

The novel that you are about to read will hit close to home... perhaps your neighborhood or next-door neighbor. Some of the events will be shocking; nevertheless, as real as life. Many of these things are going on in your own community right now. The TRAGEDY is not prostitution...But when sins of this magnitude take over an entire church and community.

FIRST WORDS

Many people who read this book will think that I am blatantly and overtly criticizing the Church. That is certainly NOT my intent. **My purpose in writing this book is to allow you the freedom to think and to admit that changes are indeed needed in our society, especially in the Church and our families.** We need to communicate more. We need to cast out the two-by-four that is in our own eye before we can see how to cast out the splinter from our neighbor's eye. We need to have more compassion and be more caring, regardless of a person's past. Any fool can criticize…and most fools do.

This is not a sex book, **but it is a book about sex, passion, lies, sins, murder, intrigue, and other issues of morality found within our society and the Church.** The following stories allow you to see what has been going on for decades behind closed doors in our communities, especially the church. How do I know? For one thing, I have been there. Almost all of these scenes are true. As previously stated, I have changed the names and places to protect the guilty. I am extremely familiar with the church scene. Actually, anyone involved in the Church today…could have written this book. As you know, the Church is not infallible. You have read and/or seen the situations within the Church in the past three decades. It's not a pretty scene. All denominations have had their problems.

***

Someone asked, "What is the secret in dealing with desperate and lonely housewives?" Let's take a look at what some people have said:

- Since women are by nature very romantic and sexy creatures, what is the secret? Women want romance. Women desire romance. Women desire sex...a lot of sex. Romance to a woman is like fresh air in the springtime or like the aromatic fragrance from a well-kept rose garden. Women are by nature...romantic, beautiful, incredible, and sensuous. Men could not live without women. They would be helpless without women. That's a fact.

- Women are the most beautiful creations that God ever made...not man, but women! They are not as desperate as some have portrayed them to be. Even though some do lead lives that do not have the romance, passion, or intimacy in which they desire, does this mean that they are **ALWAYS** actively looking for another man? No. Do they sometimes look for another man? Yes. Does this make them desperate? No. They want love and companionship.

- Even though, Americans still condemn adultery, they are among the most adulterous people on Planet Earth. Some say that...currently, 60% of married couples are in an adulterous relationship (either mentally or physically). A large part of our society and economy thrives on adultery...which includes hotels, motels, travel rendezvous, gifts, websites, clubs, movies, favorite vacation spots, and the beat goes on...

- Even politicians, pastors, priests, teachers, public officials, orators, and almost anyone you can imagine...has engaged in adultery at some point...even if it is only in their minds.

- Desperate and lonely housewives are not new to the American or global culture. As I said earlier, even in Biblical times…relationships with desperate housewives existed in many nations.
- Another Secret: Discretion and absolute trust must be in the equation process.

One person said, "Difficult and bad marriages do exist. Many men have even expressed a desire to marry a desperate and lonely housewife who may be in a bad marriage." Remember, men are as desperate as women are when it comes to companionship.

BOTTOM LINE

Even though this is a novel, much truth will be found on every page. Sins within our communities and churches come in all sizes and packages. Some people will prostitute themselves for a song...others for much more. Nonetheless, in this novel you will find all the ingredients that encompass prostitution in our communities and churches...such as...greed, thirst for power, wickedness, adultery, selfishness, lies, sexual depravity, and all sorts of other deviant behavior.

True BOTTOMLINE: There is nothing new under the sun. It stands to reason that if prostitution was found in the first book of the Bible some 6000 years ago, it would still be found in the church today...and it is.

Chapter 1
THE SEXY and SEDUCTIVE CHOIR DIRECTOR

The First Church on Blue Street in Waterford, USA is a typical southern church in the Bible belt of America. The Bible is taught every Sunday and throughout the week. The 650 parishioners are a mixture of middle class America to include blue collar, white collar, and all in between. The town of Waterford is a sleepy little giant that has a lot of energetic, bored, and sex crazy people who are very rapidly getting antsy and tense. They want more out of life...but exactly what...they have no idea. Then enters the Blue Street Sultry and Sensuous Choir Director who is incredibly beautiful, tall, slender, big-breasted and blonde...Read on.

Jack Spillane is a brilliant young college student who has everything going for him. He is tall and handsome. He is the Class President and...in general, just about everybody likes him. His grades are excellent. His future looks bright ahead...Then, he begins singing in the choir at The First Church on Blue Street.

Jack was still trying to find himself. He had given up on the church of his parents and had been going to the Blue Street Church for about a month. One Sunday morning during the worship hour, all parishioners were given a lengthy questionnaire to complete and drop in the offering plate as soon as possible. Since Jack had sung in the choir in his previous church and was presently involved in college drama and music, he decided to sign up for the Church Choir. He had no idea of what was about to happen.

A few weeks later, immediately after choir rehearsal, Mrs. Julie Brown (the attractive, energetic, hot, and blue-eyed blonde choir director) asked Jack to stay around for a few minutes. She wanted to talk to him about PRIVATE lessons…chorus lessons of course.

"Jack, how long have you been singing?"

"Mrs. Brown, I've been singing in church since I was a small boy."

"Please, don't call me Mrs. Brown. You can call me Julie. I'm not old fashioned. Most of the time, I feel like I'm sixteen again, especially when I'm around someone as handsome and sexy as you. You light up my fire…if you know what I mean. Do you get my drift, Jack?"

By now, Jack was almost speechless, but he managed to mutter, "Well…thank…you Mrs., I mean Julie. I really do not know what to say…except, you are a nice looking woman…I mean…you are very beautiful."

Julie Brown could see his innocence and embarrassment, so she responded, "Why, thank you Jack. That is so sweet of you. Look…what I really wanted to talk to you about…is this. I believe you have great singing potential, ability, and a good ear for music. With some of my private tutoring and coaching, you will become a tremendous gospel soloist. Therefore, if your schedule permits, this Saturday afternoon, let's get together at my house for your first private lesson. I'll call you later for the time and directions to our home. My husband is away on business this weekend, but that will be OK because the first lesson won't take long. See you then…Okay?"

Without the slightest clue, Jack said, "Sure…I'll see you then."

For the next couple of days, Jack's college schedule was hectic. He was now in his third year and the science courses seemed to get more difficult each semester. He was so busy until he had forgotten all about his conversation with Mrs. Brown.

On Friday evening, the telephone rang. "Is that you, Jack? How is my star singer doing?"

Jack recognized her voice. He replied, "Mrs. Brown…I mean Julie, yes, I'm doing fine. I've had a few busy days, but everything is cool."

"Good then, I'll see you tomorrow. Let's make it 2 PM. Is that good for you, Jack?"

"Yes, sounds good."

"And Jack, I live at 786 Oak Street. I'll See you about 2…and don't be late."

The next morning Jack called his girlfriend, Susie Jones, and told her that he would pick her up at 7 PM that evening. They planned to go to the movies at the shopping mall. They had been going steady for about a year. They had only recently gotten passionate with each other…but no real sex yet.

The afternoon was humid. The sky was deep blue without a cloud in sight. A gentle breeze was blowing through the tall oak trees. Jack arrived at 786 Oak Street at 2 PM sharp. He rang the door bell and waited. Nothing happened. He rang the door bell again. This time he could hear movement in the house, but did not see anyone. The front door opened. Julie was dressed to kill. She was wearing a short-short white skirt and a navy-blue type blouse with the top three buttons unbuttoned. Her breasts were almost hanging out of her bra. Her make-up was fresh and bright. Her lips were ruby red. "Come on in, Jack. Sorry, but I was in the bedroom getting dressed when I saw your car pull up," Julie explained.

As Jack came into the foyer, he said, "No problem, I'm normally early anyway. And I'm so excited about my singing and getting training…from someone like you…who has so much to offer. You look great."

"Well, thank you, my dear Jack. I do have a lot to offer and you certainly know how to make a sexy woman feel good about herself. Look, sit down and get comfortable. I'll get us some lemonade."

In a few moments, Julie returned with some tall glasses of ice-cold lemonade…spiked with a little vodka filled with ice cubes and slices of lemon.

She said, "Ok Jack, let's see what you can do. Come with me to the piano. I'll play. You sing. Let's start with the classy one 'You Are My Light'. Do you know that one?"

"Yes indeed. Play it in C. I love that song."

Jack Spillane sang his heart out for the next thirty minutes or so. Mrs. Brown gave him several more glasses of lemonade and positive feedback and only minor correction. Finally, she said, "Let's take a break. I'll get some more ice-cold lemonade. Sit down on the sofa and relax for a few minutes."

Julie returned with the delicious cold lemonade spiked with more Vodka. She handed Jack his refill. She then sat down beside him.

"Jack, do you mind if I ask you a personal question? Do you have many girlfriends?"

"Not really. Susie and I have been going together for about a year though. She is a year younger than I am...but we have a lot in common."

"Well, tell me something, Jack. You have such big arms, legs, thighs, and a tight rear-end. Does Susie like your body? Or are you still a virgin?"

"Pardon me, Mrs. Brown. What...What are you saying?"

"Are you still a virgin? Have you ever been with a woman before? You know...slept with a woman? Fooled around with a woman? Had sex with a woman?"

"Oh...no...Not really. I've made out before, but not actually going all the way. My parents always taught against that sort of thing."

"Then you really do not know what its like to have passionate sex with a desperate and wild woman, do you? I mean...to really have excitement and passion in your life...to be with a woman that wants you...desires you...that wants to have sex with you. Jack, do you get my message?"

Jack's face turned burgundy red and hot. "Julie, you are an incredibly attractive and beautiful woman, but are you sure you want to do this thing? I mean, you are a married woman and I am young enough to be your son."

Julie responded, "Jack, Jack...you are so naïve...but after today, you will be a real man!"

That day, Mr. Jack Spillane lost his innocence to the sultry and sensuous Church Choir Director. By the way, she continues to be the number one choir director in The First Church on Blue Street. None of the men objects.

Chapter 2
THE EVANGELIST

A few weeks later Jack Spillane met with the Reverend Mr. Abraham Black, the senior pastor of The First Church on Blue Street. In confidence, Jack shared with Pastor Black what had happened that afternoon with Mrs. Julie Brown. "She just came onto me like lightning. Her hands were all over me...everywhere...in my shirt...my pants...my hair...my face, my body. She went wild. It happened so fast. And Pastor...God forgive me, but I'm guilty as sin. I knew it was wrong, but the die had been cast. I was vulnerable. I was horny. I was just too weak to make a stand...and by God, I enjoyed it." Jack confessed.

"My son, don't stop there. Go on. After all, confession is good for the soul. What else happened on that steamy and hot afternoon? You have spiked my full attention."

"Well Pastor Black, the rest is history. We had passionate, wild sex and I lost my virginity. Of course...now and then, I fantasize about it. Is that wrong? What do I do? I mean, this woman looks like a movie star and is built like a #$%@!...Well, you know what I mean."

"Son, I do know what you mean. I have been there many times, but only in my mind. You must pray very hard and take lots of cold showers. And if she calls you, you call me. I will take care of the situation myself. By the way, we are starting our annual revival next week. The evangelist is an excellent speaker. I believe you will profit from his sermons."

"OK, Pastor...Thanks. I'll see you Sunday morning."

On Sunday morning, the Reverend Mr. Black preached another fiery message about hell and the evils of sin, especially adultery. He could see the smiling face of Mrs. Julie Brown sitting in the choir. Some day he would have to have a long talk with her and see what was making her tick, but not now. The revival would start that evening.

Many new converts were added to the church the following Sunday. The revival was being categorized as a tremendous success.

The evangelist, Reverend Harry Dock, was a colorful and flashy individual who wore flamboyant and glitzy clothes...and even a little make-up. He could have you crying one minute and laughing the next. The people loved him. Sometimes he was loud. Other times, he was soft spoken. And my, my...how he could quote fiery scriptures!

So the time had come for the last night of the revival. At the close of the service, the evangelist said, "Tonight, after the service, I'll be going on to Savannah. If there are any young men here that are contemplating...going into the ministry or would like to learn more about the ministry, you are welcome to join me for a few days at my next appointment."

After church, Jack Spillane talked with Evangelist Dock for several minutes. Bottomline...Jack decided to go with him for a couple of days. For one thing, the past few days had meant a lot to Jack. The preaching had made him feel good about himself and his soul again. He had received forgiveness for his sexual sins. He felt clean again.

Jack said goodbye to his girlfriend, Susie Jones, and to some of his fellow choir members. The evangelist, Reverend Harry Dock, expressed his appreciation to the Senior Pastor and board members for the large generous gift and gratuity that he had received. And then they were off...

Evangelist Dock and Jack drove about seventy-five miles. It was getting late; therefore, Reverend Harry said, "We might as well get a room for the night. We'll drive on in tomorrow and meet Pastor Slim Johnson of The First Church on Bay Road. Meanwhile, we need to get some rest."

***

Reverend Dock said that they would share a room in order to economize. After getting a room with two double beds at the Blue Ridge Motel, Jack fell asleep almost immediately. About 3 AM, he was abruptly awakened by someone or something rubbing against his legs, thighs, and private areas. The next thing he knew, someone was hugging him. Jack jumped up and shouted, "What the world is going on?"

He turned on the light and to his surprise and astonishment...there was the Reverend Harry Dock...in the nude...trying to put the make on him.

Jack immediately started putting his clothes on.

"What are you doing, Jack. I just thought we'd have a little fun. I didn't mean to upset you," the evangelist proclaimed.

Jack replied, "Look, I know you are a preacher and you probably get lonely at times, but don't ever touch me again. I'm certainly no angel. Neither am I gay. I am straight. You have your own lifestyle, but stay away from me."

"All right…all right. I'm sorry. I did not mean to frighten or offend you, Jack. I just thought…"

"Well, you thought wrong. I am so surprised at you, Reverend. I'm sorry, but I'm leaving now. I have my clothes. I'll catch a ride back home."

As Jack was leaving, the evangelist tried to give him a hundred dollar bill; nevertheless, he refused it and ran out the door.

Weeks past. Once again, Jack found himself back in the office of the Reverend Mr. Abraham Black. "There I was minding my own business…sleeping and trying to get some rest. I cannot believe things like this happen to me. Everyone here at Blue Street just loved Evangelist Dock and his preaching. How did he turn out that way? No offense, but do you think he has always been gay?"

"My son, there are many things that we do not understand in this life. What Harry Dock did in frightening you was not right. But we must forgive him. He is in God's Hands. I am sorry that you were startled and had to experience something like this against your will. Hopefully, Reverend Black will get some counseling and psychological therapy in dealing with himself and others when it comes to his own sexuality."

Chapter 3
THE SCAM

The First Church on Blue Street was beginning to "bust out" at the seams. They were now having three services on Sunday mornings to accommodate the large crowds. Everyone seemed to just love the Reverend Mr. Black until...

Apparently, two of his elders (Joseph Pine and Timothy Little) had been stirring up strife among the membership. The word from the grapevine was..."Pastor Black is just too sympathetic toward people and favors the younger crowd too much. He wants change. He talks about change all the time. He needs to preach more 'fire and brimstone' sermons. He's getting too soft. He is getting too close to the people."

Both Pine and Little said. "We as elders know what is best for this congregation. We have been in this church a long, long time. We know what is good for these people."

For the next three months, they said all kinds of nasty things behind Pastor Abraham Black's back. They accused him of "wanting change" and being too soft, too insensitive, and not being in touch with his parishioners. But, no one paid any attention to their accusations until...

One Sunday evening after the short service, Elders Pine and Little met at Martha's Diner.

"Look here, Joe. We're losing our power over this congregation. They think Pastor Black is some kind of saint. We must stop this character from being such a strong figure with this local assembly. After all, we've been here for them over twenty years. Who does this Black fellow think he is?" asked Tim.

Elder Joseph Pine responded, "I'll tell you what we are going to do. We are going to call in one of our markers. Jill St Cloud, the lovely and lonely brunette with the beautiful body...owes us a couple of favors. Remember the night she was caught in bed with Deacon Jones when her husband was out of town on business? We can call in a favor. Listen, here's what we'll do..."

The following week, Elder Pine met secretly with the desperate, lusty, and robust Mrs. Jill St Cloud in the Wall Mart parking lot. As they were sitting in her Park Avenue Buick, Pine said, "Listen, we need a favor from you. As you know, right now we are having difficulties with the Reverend Mr. Black. He has gotten too big for his pants. He is gaining too much influence and power in our little town of Waterford. The people are placing too much confidence in him. This has got to cease. Who does he think he is? We run this town...not him."

"What do you want me to do?" asked Jill.

"Well, you're a beautiful, sexy, and voluptuous woman. You figure it out. And by the way, this meeting never happened. Okay?"

"I believe I get the picture. After I do this shady favor for you and Tim, I want you to leave me and my family alone. What's in the past is in the past. This blackmail and non-sense have gone far enough. Do you get my drift?"

"Yes. Don't worry about it. Your secret is safe with us forever! You just repay our favor, you hear?"

***

In a few days, the beautiful Jill St Cloud called the pastor.

"Pastor Black, I have a personal problem. I need your help. I need your professional advice. Can you come over, perhaps tomorrow morning? I'll have coffee and donuts ready when you get here. We'll talk about it then. I can't talk to you on the phone about it. It's too sensitive."

"Tomorrow is not a good time for me, Mrs. St Cloud. What about 9 AM on Thursday morning? But forget the donuts. I do not need the fat pills. OK?"

"That'll be fine with me. I'll be ready for you. See you then."

The Reverend Mr. Black didn't have a clue as to what was about to happen. He had never dealt with anything like this before. He was not a saint, but was a man of integrity and goodness. But now, through no fault of his own, his reputation was all about to take a nosedive and his life would never be the same again. He was about to be had.

Pastor Black dropped by the church office on Thursday morning for a few minutes to listen to his voicemail. He told his secretary, Mrs. Jody Brown, that he was scheduled to counsel with Mrs. St Cloud for a few minutes at her home and would return in about an hour.

At 8:55 AM, when he arrived at Jill St Cloud's home, everything seemed normal. The aroma of the freshly cut lawn, the
beautiful flower garden, and fresh coffee were especially notice-
able. The morning paper was still in the driveway. To be courte-
ous, Pastor Black picked up the paper to give to Jill when she
opened the door.

He rang the door bell. Jill, still dressed in her scanty, deep
red housecoat, opened the door and invited him in.

"Listen, Jill...Maybe now is not a good time to talk to you
about your problem. You're still dressed in your nightclothes."

"Oh, I'm sorry. Maybe this would be better..."

She turned and immediately took off her bright red, silk
robe. To the pastor's surprise, she had nothing on underneath.
She was completely naked. Before he knew what was happening,
she grabbed him with both hands and laid a lip lock on him. She
also fondled his private parts. He squirmed and wriggled until he
got free.

"What the world is the matter with you? Are you mad? You
are a married woman. I'm a married man. We are Christians. I am
the pastor of The First Church on Blue Street. You are a parishioner. What you have just done is wrong. It's very wrong. Tell me,
what's going on here?"

As she quickly put her robe back on, she said, "Pastor Black,
I don't know what came over me. Please forgive me. I'm sorry. As
you probably know, my husband and I have not been getting along
lately, especially in the sex arena...Now, I'm sex starved. I need a
fix. Again, I'm very sorry."

"Listen, young lady, you both need help. I suggest you call my secretary and make an appointment. Next time, make sure you bring your husband with you because under no circumstances… will I counsel you alone. I'll see my own self out."

On the way back to the church, the Reverend Mr. Black could not believe what had just happened to him. "The whole world has gone crazy," he thought.

Meanwhile, back at Jill St Cloud's, the plot thickens. The two elders (Pine and Little) who had been parked down the street… were now at Jill's planning the next strategic step in their ploy and reprehensible, culpable, and evil deeds.

"OK, OK, I got everything on video tape. You can edit the tape anyway you like. Here's the tape. Now go and don't ever bother me again. Get the heck out of my house. You hear? You two "so called" elders make me sick at my stomach. Pastor Black is a noble and good man."

About this time, Elder Little said, "You shut your little lousy mouth, you slut. Remember who's holding the goods on you? And don't you dare get smart with us, you worthless hussy and @#$%&. We know that you slept with Deacon Jones. We have the goods on you. Shut your face. Do you hear me?"

In a very loud voice, Jill replied, "You've got what you want… now get out of my house."

The two elders went back to their car and sped away.

A couple of weeks past and just two days before the next church board meeting, Pine and Little made an appointment with the pastor.

"How are you two doing?" asked Pastor Black.

Elder Pine responded, "We're doing great; however, we didn't come here to talk about us. We came here to talk about your situation. We have warned you several times in the past year to tighten up...to stop trying to bring about change and catering to the young people. We have given you suggestions about what we wanted you to preach...but no, you have done things your own way. You have not listened to anything we have said. It's like you are deaf or something. Well, that's all coming to a rapid close now. We want your resignation or..."

"Or you'll do what. Don't you know there are eight other men on the board? And even then, it takes 3/4's majority vote of the congregation to force me to resign," said Pastor Black.

"Black, I guess you think we are stupid or something. Do we look stupid to you? Do you think we are brain dead? We were not born yesterday. We have been in the way (the Bible Way) for a long time. People respect us around here. This is our town. We own it and own most of the people here. We have tremendous influence in this town. The people trust us," Little said.

With a smirk on his face, Pine shook his fist in the pastor's face and said, "We've finally got you...you little rascal and stupid jack. Your little game is up. You see this video in my hand? Let me show you something, you nit-wit and #$%^&."

The shady and unscrupulous elders brought in the DVD, which they had tampered with. They put it in the DVD player and began to play it. The show began. It showed Pastor Black kissing a naked lady in whom it was quite evident, was not his wife. Special audio effects had been added for effect. Here he was...kissing a nude woman, breathing profusely, and making passionate sounds.

Black responds, "So this is what's going on. This is the lowest scheme of depravity that I have ever seen in my entire life. You two men need to repent of your wicked deeds. This is outrageous, scandalous, contemptible, and disgraceful. You two are evil men. If you don't repent, you're going straight to hell. You will not pass "go". You will not receive $200. Do you hear me?"

Little replied, "We concur that we are evil. We concur that we are somewhat depraved. We concur that we are scandalous. With that being established...This is the deal and only deal that you will get. In two days, you are going to resign. Because if you don't, the entire town will see this video. Then, what will you do? You better start cleaning out your desk right away...You know what I mean? You should have listened to us earlier. No, you wanted to have it your way. Well, now your time is up."

Pastor Black said, "You two guys are full of deceitfulness, dishonesty, and debauchery. You're not honorable men. You know in your hearts that the video is a lie. I'm not perfect. I'm a sinner saved by grace, but I would never do anything as despicable as what you have suggested. I love my family, this church, community, and town too much for this sort of thing."

"We totally agree with you. We admire you. You are a good man...an honorable man. Apparently, you don't get the message.

This is not about whether you are a good man or not. That's immaterial. We want you out of here. We lost control of this congregation about a year ago…and we now want it back. Therefore, we are doing just that…taking back what belongs to us. Goodbye, Mr. Abraham Black," said Joseph Pine.

Two days later, one hour before the church board meeting, the Reverend Mr. Abraham Black…better known as an honorable man and one of the founding pastors of The First Church on Blue Street in the quiet town of Waterford…shot himself with a borrowed .357 magnum. He died instantly. The community went into shock. He left no suicide note. People everywhere were asking, "What happened? Why would he do such a thing? I cannot believe he is gone."

Chapter 4

THE BREWING OF A HOT LOVE AFFAIR

Several days later at Pastor Black's funeral, the chief elder (Mr. Joseph Pine) and his partner in crime (Mr. Timothy Little), participated in Black's eulogy. With tears in his eyes, Pine said. "This man was above reproach. He was kind, honest, and had a heart for the people. This tragic event will have an effect upon each of us in this city for a long time to come. I cannot believe he's gone. He was like a father to us. This is such a misfortune. He was such a wonderful man and pastor!"

With handkerchief in hand, Little said, "We have lost a true hero...a man of integrity and dignity. And as all of you know, our grievous loss is heaven's gain. He will never again suffer pain or grief or sorrow. To this great man of statue, we salute and say, 'Farewell, good soldier, farewell'".

The following Friday at noon, Elders Pine and Little met at their favorite gossip center, Martha's Diner, for lunch. "Well, life must go on. You know, the Assistant Pastor, Johnny Tune is a pretty good old boy. He's one of us. Now that he's the Senior Pastor, we can run this church the way that we know best. After all, who knows this congregation better than we do? You and I have been here a long, long time. We know what's best for these people," replied Pine.

"You're absolutely right, Joe. I believe we can work with Tune. He seems to have his head screwed on right. He is younger and talks our language, too. He likes money, luxury cars, fancy clothes, nice homes, golf, a little gambling, and beautiful, sexy women. He has an unholy animosity for the Welfare Programs of this country. He thinks that our taxes are too high. He does not like Social Security taxes or Federal taxes. He does not like foreign investments. He likes products made in America. And he thinks the present Washington Administration needs some serious discipline and restraint."

They continued to plan their strategy over the lunch hour. Suddenly, Pine asked, "But what about his wife, Tamie Tune? Isn't she one of those right wing liberals that preaches Women's Lib? She is always saying obnoxious things about nothing. In addition, she does not like men."

Little: "Well, she does like men because lately, she has been giving me more than the right hand of fellowship. She smiles at me and even winks at me in a sexy way from time to time. She even hugged me tightly the other day. I think she wants me."

Pine: "Get out of here, you sly dog. You're not saying what I think, are you? Are you saying she has the "hots" for you?"

Little: "Yes, I am, Joe. She has the hots for me...I can feel it. I see it in her eyes. I see it in her expressions. She wants me."

Pine: "Well, if that's true, please use discretion. After all, you are one of the chief elders of The First Church on Blue in beautiful downtown Waterford. Be careful."

***

Two months later in one of the adult Sunday School classes, a heated discussion centered on the topic "Women in the Home". Some of the men got real upset with Tamie Tune, the wife of the Senior Pastor (Johnny Tune). Read on...

Her philosophy gave vent to several concepts that rubbed some of the men the wrong way. For example, Tamie said, "I believe a woman should have the right to pursue a career if she so desires. If she does work outside the home, then her husband should share in the responsibilities of home chores...dishes...laundry...making beds...and other duties as required. On the other hand, I do not believe that a woman should have to go out and get a job unless she chooses to do so. In this case, the husband should make a decent living for his family and wife. The problem that I have seen in this generation is...some men are slothful, lazy, no-good, and just plain loafers. Some men are just too lazy to hold a good job."

Tensions were high. The discussion was heated until the teacher (Elder Timothy Little) had to dismiss the class early before a fight broke out.

As everyone was leaving, Little asked, "Could I speak with you a moment, Mrs. Tune?"

Tamie: "Of course you can. I would just love to talk with you for awhile...you good looking man."

Tim: "Listen, you were pretty rough on the men, weren't you? They are from the old school. Most of them think that a woman should be seen and not heard. I can tell you right now... you did not make any new friends among the men today. And the next thing they will do is…ostracize you and forbid their wives from speaking with you. They will shun you".

Tamie: "OK, OK. Tell me something, then. Where do you stand in all of this? Are you a man or are you one of the wimps around here? I'd like to see a real man with a real backbone and testes. Do you get my drift?"

A few minutes later in Worship Service, Tune and Little really looked each other over during the preaching of the sermon by Pastor Johnny Tune. He preached his heart out on that hot and unforgettable morning. The subject: "Adultery, Prostitution, and Power."

Quite paradoxical and ironic, wouldn't you agree? Two days later, the two incorrigibles and shameless church members began a steamy, passionate, and burning love affair! They began making passionate love all over town in every motel, park, and wooded areas in Waterford. What started as a one-night stand became a never-ending erotic love affair that lasted for several months.

Joseph Pine and Timothy Little continued to meet weekly at Martha's Diner. "How is it going?" asked Joe.

Tim replied, "It's going good, but Tamie won't leave me alone! I don't want to hurt her feelings, but I am worn out from all this steamy sex. I need some peace and relaxation from all this excitement. Do you get my drift?"

Joe replied, "Tim, you are dealing with a desperate house-wife. Furthermore, you are acting desperate as well. You are losing your objectivity. Desperation is making you react in an extreme fashion. Tamie has pushed all of your hot buttons. You are rapidly becoming a man out of control. You need to lighten up and be sensitive to your own feelings as well as hers. You need to relax and realize that this affair is only temporary. I know you care for her, but I believe you have gone over the edge. I also know that you have been very hard on yourself for this burning and passionate love affair. You feel guilty as sin. Accept yourself as you are. You like to fool around. Accept it. Now, you are beginning to blame yourself and Tamie. Stop this affair before it gets the best of you."

A few days later, Tim secretly went to their normal rendezvous point. To his surprise, guess what? Mr. Joe Pine (his friend and fellow elder) was already there...in the nude making love to guess who? You are right...Mrs. Tamie Tune. Can you believe this? She is making love to two Church Leaders at the same time.

Chapter 5
THE STEAMY LOVE AFFAIR

Tuesday morning in Waterford seemed to begin like any other morning for a small southern town. The temperature at 7 AM was 72 degrees and the humidity was 85%. Rain was in the forecast. Traffic was moderate. Things seemed so peaceful and normal. Tranquility was in the air.

Pastor Tune awoke about 6:30...got up...got dressed...ate some Corn Flakes...and took off for another adventurous and intrepid day at The First Church on Blue Street.

For Tamie Tune, it was another story...a different story. Since she had switched her lover from Timmy Little to Joe Pine, she finally thought she was in love. She had incredible plans for the day.

She got out of bed whistling and singing. She was all excited about having coffee with Elder Joe Pine. Her mind was wandering restlessly. She had thought about Joe at least a dozen times in the past 24 hours and even fantasized about him. She thought he was sexy, passionate, and handsome. She kept thinking, "I think I am falling in love with this guy."

At 10:15 AM as Tamie and Joe were having coffee at Martha's Diner, Tamie asked, "Well, are you a real man?"

Joe: "What's that, Tamie?"

Tamie: "Are you a real man or a mouse? I know that we have been intimate and I believe you are a real man, but are you going to be a wimp like Elder Timothy Little and leave me to be alone by myself? I cannot stand to be alone."

Joe: "First, let me ask you a question, Tamie. What is your definition of a real man?"

Tamie: "Do you really want to know?"

Joe: "Yes, I really want to know. I really do...once and for all...I want to know. What is a real man?"

Tamie: "OK, big guy...follow me home in your car and I'll show you what a real man is."

Joe: "Tamie, do you have any respect for your husband... the Pastor of The First Church on Blue Street? Have you lost all decency and virtue? We are talking about your home."

Tamie: "What's the matter? Am I too hot, sexy, and passionate for you to handle? Do you have the balls or not? You do find me attractive, don't you?"

Joe: "Yes, extremely. You are slim, trim, sexy, beautiful, and tremendously desirable. Are you sure you want to go through with this in your home?"

Tamie: "Yes...and don't you dare disappoint me, little man. Okay?"

They arrived about 11:00 AM and went inside immediately. As Tamie stood up, she said, "Let's do it and let's do it now. We do not have time to waste standing around and shooting the breeze with small talk."

Thus began a two-year love affair that ended only when Tamie got pregnant…and eventually had an abortion by an out of state doctor.

Meanwhile though, they continued to have trysts and sexual rendezvous all over the county. They also went to Joe's mountain cabin and traveled together on several convention trips. They seemed to be consumed with adulterated lust. Because of their extracurricular activities, they each lost fifteen pounds in four weeks.

During the two year lustful affair, they both continued their Sunday School class discussions every Sunday morning with about fifty others in attendance. Elder Little taught the adult class as a learned theologian and Mrs. Tune sat on the front row and stirred up the people with her liberalized views on everything from abortion to homosexuality to euthanasia. Many times she would go on a "man bashing" spree and had a lot of fun doing it. Most of the men would get fighting mad, but do nothing.

However, one time…not only did a fervent and sizzling discussion develop, but also a fistfight broke out in the middle of the classroom.

Tamie started the ruckus when she said, "I think we ought to go out and start feeding all the homeless in this town. They really need our help. Some so-called members of this church only think of themselves. And some others even think the homeless are just scum and the lowest form of life. Well, let me tell you something…It's an indictment against this church. Some of these helpless souls could go to hell."

"Now, you hold on there, Tamie. That's a big fat lie. As a deacon of this church, we are doing something. Currently, we are providing three lunches a week for the homeless and every once and awhile, we give out shoes," replied Deacon Jones.

Deacon Charles Berry spoke up, "Jones, you're out of line. Don't you be calling the Pastor's wife a liar, you hear? She may be a lot of things, but she is not a liar. Show some respect."

"You shut your face, you little liberal. This stupid woman comes in this class and causes nothing but trouble every Sunday… and everybody knows it, especially you. This used to be a great Sunday School Class, but now, we constantly argue," screamed Jones.

Suddenly, without warning, Jones received a blow to his head and stomach and the fight was on between Berry and Jones. Pow… scratch, bang, boom, crash, whack, punch, and #$%^&* were the sounds that came exploding from inside the hot little room in the educational plant of The First Church on Blue Street.

Eventually, the fight was stopped…but only after Jones took a folding chair and hit Berry in the back. Both were hurt…Berry critically. An ambulance came and hauled both of them away to Mercy Hospital.

Afterwards, Tamie Tune said, "Well, sometimes men will be men and act like little boys. After all, men are just boys grown up.

Well, some have grown up. Most of them around here will never grow up because they are stupid."

She smiled...got in her Black Mercedes...waved through the tinted window and drove off.

Chapter 6
THE TEMPTATION

Several months passed. The church was growing. People were giving faithfully in the offerings. A time of healing and peaceful bliss were focusing on the minds of the parishioners. They seemed to be enjoying themselves more than ever before, even in the midst of the lean and weak economy (recession). People seemed to be more open and honest than usual. It was time for another revival...

Evangelist Bobby Shell arrived on Saturday afternoon. He was welcomed by several of the deacons and elders. Pastor Johnny Tune was out of town on a speaking engagement. He was scheduled to return the following morning...in time to kick off the first service of the three-day revival.

Meantime, Elder Dale Dickens escorted the evangelist to the Holiday Inn and got him settled in his room.

"Listen, one of the staff members will pick you up in the van tomorrow morning...about 7:45 AM for the first service. You are scheduled to speak at all three services. See you tomorrow. If you need anything, call the church office or the other number I gave you earlier," Elder Dickens said loudly.

"Okay, see you later", responded Shell.

The evening was progressing very nicely when Evangelist Shell heard a knock at his door.

"Now, who could that be?" he thought to himself.

Shell opened the door. There stood a beautiful, extremely sexy, sultry, attractive young lady with deep blue eyes and long blonde hair.

"Can I come in?" she asked.

"Certainly, you may. Here, sit right over there by the TV. What's up?"

"You don't know me. My name is Mary O'Leary. I'm on the Welcome Committee for the church. I just dropped by to see if you needed anything...anything at all. After all, you are on the road a lot, away from your wife and family...and I'm sure you get lonely at times. Therefore, with that said, if I can be of any assistance, anything at all, you let me know."

"What did you have in mind, Ms. O'Leary?"

"Well...perhaps, you may need a massage or a rubdown while you're here in our wonderful city. Perhaps, you may want me to draw your bath water...or even take a bath with you for companionship. Or if you are lonely at night or anytime, let me know. I have just the cure for that. If you need anything...anything at all...just feel free to let me know. I'm available night or day. I'm at your beckoning call. OK? And please, you can call me Sister Mary."

"Thanks for the candid offer, Sister Mary. If I need anything while I'm here in Waterford, I'll call you. Goodnight, my dear."

For the next few nights, Evangelist Shell preached some rather hellfire and brimstone sermons. The people liked him. The deacons liked him. The elders even liked him…and Mary O'Leary certainly liked him and wanted him sexually. "He was hot", she thought.

***

He managed to call his lovely wife and children every day. He even wrote her a poem and faxed it to her one morning. It was called:

"**The Godly Wife and Mother**"

Sweetheart, as my wonderful Wife, you are very SPECIAL to me.
You have given me warmth when I have been cold.
At times, I have been too anxious about things, but you have been so bold.
At times, I have been weak with my strength almost gone,
But YOU have always been so strong.
I had a fever on my brow,
You came and comforted me and prayed.
A beautiful smile came over your face
When you saw the Lord's amazing grace.

As the Mother of our children, you are SPECIAL.
Our children really love you.
While I'm away, please get some well-deserved rest.
Your fervent prayers have stood the test
Thanks for loving me and not being afraid to invest.
Hopefully, after all these years, I'm still on your mind.
You're a woman, wife, and mother after God's kind.

My Love, you make my life so wonderful and happy.
You have made me one contented husband and real fine
Dad! I love you!

***

One evening as he returned to the motel, he was not prepared for what he found. He opened the door to his suite, and
guess what? That's right. Dear Sister O'Leary was there waiting
for him.

Bobby: "What are you doing here? Who let you into my
room? Look, I'm a married man. You need to go right now."

Mary: "Bobby, Bobby, I thought you might want a backrub
and some company. Don't tell me you do not get lonely at times.
I don't believe that for a second. Let me give you a hot soapy
bath and a long hot massage and afterwards we'll make passionate love..."

Bobby: "Mrs. O'Leary, stop! Yes, I do get lonely at times.
Yes, you are very attractive, lovely, sexy, and beautiful. And yes...I
do like to talk to people, especially when I spend so much time
studying and being on the road. Nevertheless, you must go. You
are very seductive and attractive and it's thoughtful of you to
think about my needs. But as I stated earlier, I'm a happily married man with three wonderful children. You are a kind person. I
know your husband must really appreciate a good and benevolent
woman like you. Go, before I beg you to stay!"

Mary: "If you only knew how much I wanted you...Don't
you find me desirable? Are you saying that you don't want me?
Are you saying I'm not sexy? What are you saying?"

Bobby: "Mrs. Mary, it's quite the contrary and diametrically the opposite; however, as I have now repeated for a third time, I…Rev. Bobby Shell, am a faithful and contented and happily married man who adores his wife very much. I must now say 'GOOD-BYE' to you, Mary O'Leary."

Mary: "Then, you do desire me, but you'd rather remain faithful to your wife?"

Bobby: "Exactly…You are very, very attractive. You have raised my body temperature by at least 4 degrees. My flesh cries out for you, but it would be so wrong for us to do such a thing. And let me say this to you in private. As a man, this has been an extremely strong temptation. If it had been at another time in my life, I don't think I would have past the exam. Now, give me that key and go before I beg you to stay."

Mary: "Okay, just one more thing, Bobby, my love. Give me a hug and a kiss and I will be on my merry way."

Unfortunately, that night Bobby Shell lowered his guard. He hugged her tight…too tight perhaps. He then kissed her once…twice…three times…and then it was all over. They went to bed together and had hot passionate sex for the next two hours. Finally, Mary had to go. She said, "Okay, I must go. If you wake up in the middle of the night and want me again, take a good cold shower. Good-Bye, my love."

Evangelist Shell would never forget this night. After Mary left, he got up and took a cold shower…not once, but twice. He had been tempted…and had failed the test. Did he regret it? No! He still fantasizes to this day about Mary O'Leary.

Chapter 7

THE GREEDY TREASURER

For many years, Deacon James Smith, a local banker had been the church treasurer. His claim to fame was his experience with money and making money. As a matter of truth, Deacon James loved money more than life itself. He was an excellent accountant and CPA; however, his downfall was the love of money and women, especially women in his church.

He would sell his own mother for a few bucks. He had tried marriage more than once, but his three ex-wives complained of his selfish, stingy, controlling, and tyrannical behavior. They each divorced him within a year or two.

For twelve years, Smith had been embezzling money from the church. He was somewhat of a genius with money schemes. He was sly as a fox. Since he donated a lot of his accounting abilities to the church as free gratis, no one would suspect or even think about one of their uptown bankers being a thief. But he was a thief of the lowest kind...stealing from the church. He was a real jerk.

One of the dastardly and depraved deeds that he prided himself in...was the scheme he used to rip-off and deceive the IRS. Every Sunday evening, he would write a check to the church for all the loose change that had been collected in all the offerings of the day, to include the Sunday School offerings and special missions' offerings. Sometimes, this could amount to a lot of money. Over a year's time, it amounted to several thousand dollars. He had told the church board that he was an avid coin collector...and loved to collect coins.

At the end of the year for tax purposes, this is what he would do: Besides the offerings that he gave as a legitimate tax write-off, he also claimed a tax credit for all the checks that he had written for the loose change. According to his tax returns, his tax-deductible contributions amounted to more than one third of his income.

Lying to the IRS was one thing, but how was he stealing from the church?

Our sly Deacon Smith had two sets of books. One set of books was the set in which the board members and any auditing or accounting firm had access to. The other set was secretly hidden away for his eyes only. He knew...right to the penny how much was actually in the church account. After all, the church's account was in his bank. He was no novice at this sort of thing and his lavish lifestyle showed it. His love for money, women, sex, and gambling was soon going to land him in jail where he would not pass "Go" or collect $200, but would in fact go to jail. But in the meantime...

Since he was an outstanding citizen of Waterford...president of a local bank...a generous contributor to the church and community, who would ever suspect this clever fox of stealing from the coffers? He was a model citizen it seemed.

However, Deacon James Smith had a big mouth. He liked to brag a lot. He loved to talk about himself and his achievements. Life was all about him. This eventually got him into big trouble.

It was the Fourth of July week-end. Deacon Smith had been to the Daytona NASCAR Race with a beautiful sexy friend, Sister Mary O'Leary...from the Welcome Committee. They had spent a passionate week-end together and were returning in his black Mercedes to the holy city of Waterford. Just outside of Savannah, they stopped at the Ramada Inn.

"We might as well spend the night here since it's getting so late. We'll drive on in tomorrow...if that's OK with you, Mary," said Smith.

"Oh, sure, that's fine with me."

After they got checked into their suite, James asked, "Mary, would you like to have a drink or two before dinner and kind of relax for a few minutes?"

"Yes, I think that would be rather nice and cozy."

They went to the Sahara Bar and Restaurant and began their evening of fun, food, fellowship, martinis, screwdrivers, gen and tonics, jokes, sex, and revelry. The night was young. Smith felt like talking. He could not resist talking about himself. He let his guard down and initiated the following conversation.

"Mary, I enjoy your company. I really do. You are sexy and incredibly beautiful. You and I have a lot in common and even share some of the same goals. We both have expensive taste. We like a high standard of living...the finer things...expensive homes, luxury cars, jewelry, expensive coats, and we like to make out. Not only do we enjoy money, but we also like what money will buy."

"Well, Jim, I'll tell you something. You will always be my friend. You are highly intelligent. You are unselfish and kind. You go to church on a regular basis. You have made personal sacrifices in order to give up a lot of your time to be a deacon and the Treasurer of our Church...and above all, you're excellent in bed."

"Speaking about the Office of Treasurer...you know, I believe I have done a jam-up job as Treasurer for the past twelve years. Did you know that every year...we have an outside audit...and for the last twelve years, they have not found one error? So that proves that my keeping two sets of books have actually worked and that those idiots are stupid, dumb, and completely naive..."

"What the Sam Hill are you talking about, Jim? What do you mean...two sets of books?"

"Did I say two sets of books? I meant two sets of records...I mean, two sets of strategies. Oh, never mind...I think I've had one martini too many."

"Yeah, Ok, let's get something to eat. I could go for a big delicious T-Bone steak about now," replied Mary.

"Sure, me too. Let's do it."

***

Several weeks past, but Sister Mary O'Leary from the Welcome Committee could not get it off her mind. She thought about what Deacon James Smith had said about "the two sets of books". She thought, "I may be a sex addict, but I am loyal to the church."

"Why would Jim steal from The First Church on Blue Street? He was a wealthy banker. He didn't need to steal. He had all kinds of money. Furthermore, he owned the bank. It didn't make any sense. He loved the people and church too much."

While shopping in one of the Waterford grocery stores one afternoon, Mary bumped into one of Deacon Smith's ex-wives, Susan. She knew Susan only casually, but she just had to ask her one question.

"Susan, I know you're in a hurry; however, I have a personal question I would like to ask you…that is, if it's OK."

"If it's about that selfish, deadbeat ex-husband of mine, forget it. He's now two months behind on his child support payments. He is a deadbeat ex-husband who is selfish as they come," replied Susan.

"No, that's not it. You were married to Jim about two years, weren't you?"

"Yes, two years, two months, two days, and ten hours…but who is counting?"

"Listen, did you ever hear him say anything about keeping two sets of books for the church?"

"Hmmmn, as a matter of fact, I did…but only a time or two…when Jim was drinking excessively. Jim always liked to brag about how good of an accountant he was. 'No one was ever going to find him in error,' he would say, especially after he had a few drinks."

"Susan…thanks so much. You have been very helpful…See you later."

The following Sunday morning, Mary went to see Pastor Johnny Tune in between services. "Pastor, I have a quick question. How's the money situation in this church?"

"My Dear, what on earth are you talking about?"

And for the next ten minutes, she explained to the Pastor her theory and her legitimate concerns about the church's finances.

"Mary, thank you very much for this information. I'm sure it's nothing to be alarmed about, but we'll certainly look into it the first thing tomorrow morning. OK?"

"Thank you, Pastor."

The next morning, Pastor Tune called in a friend of his, a retired detective, Andy Johnson, from Atlanta. "Andy, I need your help and professional advice. I do not think there is anything to what I'm about to tell you, but again, there might be. I must have complete confidentiality in this matter. Do you understand me?"

"Pastor, you've got it. What's up?"

"I want you to check on the finances of this church for the past ten years…contributors, amounts, dates, deposits, bills, receipts…and oh yes, I want you to check on Deacon James Smith, the Treasurer. Check his assets and bank accounts."

"Pastor, do you think Smith is stealing from the church?"

"Andy, to be perfectly honest with you, I do not. However, since you owe me so many favors, it wouldn't hurt to check it out…"

"You've got it. I'll keep you informed…See you in a few days with my initial findings."

Andy Johnson had no idea what he would find in the next ten days. He was shocked. He could not believe his own investigative results. It just blew his mind. Upon reaching conclusive evidence of embezzlement and corruption, he called the Pastor and set up a meeting.

"Let me tell you something before we get started with this, Pastor Johnny. This is big time embezzlement. Our beloved Treasurer is going straight to hell and to jail and will not pass goal. Neither will he collect two hundred dollars ever again from this church."

"Andy, what on earth are you suggesting?"

"I'm not suggesting anything…nothing but the cold facts. Mr. James Smith is a thief and a robber of the lowest kind. I have turned over every leaf and piece of dirt in this man's financial life. Did you know that he currently has assets in excess of ten million dollars? Did you also know that he gambled away over a million dollars last year? In the past ten months, he has taken three trips to Europe, each time with a different female traveling companion from Waterford. Did you know that he has four Mercedes' and several other luxury cars?"

"Andy, my dear Andy, what does this have to do with Jim and his official position as Treasurer of this church? Has he embezzled any money from us or not?"

"OK, here are the cold and calculated facts. Mr. Smith has illegally, with malice aforethought…stolen in excess of $1.5 million dollars…over the past twelve years from this holy sanctuary. He is guilty as sin…you hear me? Guilty as sin. Here are the documents to prove it."

"Let me see those documents."

Within the next 72 hours, Deacon James Smith was arrested on several charges stemming from the investigation and research initiated by Andy Johnson. All incriminating evidence and legal documents were turned over to the Waterford Police Department. They made the arrest.

Smith posted a One Hundred Thousand Dollar Bond the next day and made himself scarce around town for a while.

Then the unexpected happened. On Monday morning, he was found hanging in the vault of his own bank…with a suicide note…left on his desk…neatly written on his bank's stationary.

In short, it read as follows:

From James Smith: "You thought you had me, but by now, you know that isn't true. I'm too smart for you. You are all so stupid and dumb. I'll never spend a day in jail…perhaps in hell, But not in jail. Yes, my downfall was money and women. Money was my faithful ally, companion, and idol. It was supposed to be my servant; nonetheless, somehow that got reversed. I became its slave and it became my master. I'm so sorry that I can't stick around for the trial, but the trial would probably bore me to death. Anyway, I'll say goodbye for now…It was fun while it lasted. I'm out of here! I win again. You are all idiots."

Signed: Deacon James Smith

Hence, we cannot throw the book at Deacon Smith, but we can close this chapter on him!

Chapter 8
THE JUDAS

Waterford was bursting at the seams. New businesses and industries were coming in from out-of-state. New families were also moving in...and The First Church on Blue Street was growing dramatically. Thus begins another interesting chapter...

The scenario begins like this. Reverend Bubba Casey was next to the Senior Pastor (Johnny Tune) in authority and responsibility...as far as ministry to The First Church on Blue Street. The entire staff consisted of four full time ministers and two part time ministers and several staff assistants. People had a lot of confidence in Bubba Casey, especially since he had been dedicated and christened as a child in this very same church and later baptized in its baptistery.

For years, Pastor Tune and Casey were the best of friends until...

One scorching, blistering, and sweltering hot day, the Senior Pastor began looking for Bubba. He asked Bubba's secretary if she had seen him.

"Why, yes, I have, Pastor. He's in a counseling session with Mrs. Margie Campbell. Her session should be up in about ten minutes, though. Is there something that I can do?"

"No, no...that's all right. I just needed to talk to him for a moment, that's all."

In a few minutes, Pastor Tune went by Bubba's office door on his way to the water fountain. As he was walking by, the Pastor heard several passionate cries of ecstasy, some definite sexual overtures, and a lot of heavy breathing.

Without hesitation or batting an eye, Pastor Tune opened the door immediately and asked, "What on earth is going on in here?"

Mrs. Campbell and Bubba were going at it in the nude on the bright red sofa. Their clothes were lying next to his desk. Both were red faced and highly embarrassed. Mrs. Campbell seemed to be mortified. Bubba was speechless and trying very clumsily to get his pants on.

"Both of you get dressed and come to my office immediately. We must talk and we must talk now."

Pastor Tune went to his office with tears in his eyes. He could not believe what he had just witnessed. This was tragic in so many ways. What was he going to say? What was he going to do? Why did this happen? Pastor Tune thought, "The whole world has gone crazy. What am I to do? Bubba is like a son to me."

Bubba Casey was his right hand man. He had depended on him for years. His integrity had been above reproach...until now. He was one of the most giving, considerate, compassionate, understanding, and honest men he had ever met.

What was only about five minutes seemed like an eternity to Pastor Tune. "God, I don't know what to say to Bubba. He's been like a son to me. I'd rather die than counsel with him and Margie right now, but I know I must..."

The door opened and the two walked in with their heads bowed low, looking toward the dark blue carpet on the floor. Both were filled with remorse and sadness. They knew they had let the Pastor down. Yes, they had been sexually active for several years; but they did not mean for this to happen...to get caught!

With large tears in his eyes, Pastor Tune spoke very softly. "You two are like my very own children. I love you both. You are both fine people...wonderful people. You're hard workers in the Church. I am just appalled and dumbfounded over this type of behavior. You are both married...but to different spouses. What on earth possessed you to do such a thing, especially inside this holy edifice? I am so sorry. What should I do with you?"

Margie sobbed, "I'm guilty as sin. I deserve to go to hell, but you haven't lived with the stupid #@$%^ (jerk) that I have lived with for the past ten years. And then...came...Bubba...my sweet Bubba. He is always so kind and comforting to me. I love him and will do anything for him...anything..."

"My Darling...I love you too, but the Pastor is right. We have greatly sinned. I have broken the trust that was commissioned to me by the people. I knew better, but I was too weak to resist. Each time we made love, I vowed that it was the last time...but our indiscretions and escapades continued," said Bubba.

"How long has this been going on?" asked the Pastor.

"For about six years, now," responded Margie.

"My God, Casey...You are the Assistant Pastor. Why didn't you come to me?"

"I wanted to; yet, I enjoyed the illicit affair. I could not resist the hot and passionate sex that I was getting. I actually looked forward to it. I know I'm sick, but I'm being honest with you."

"OK, OK. Let me think about this for a few days because I do not know what the solution or ramifications are going to be…but let me warn you right now. You two stay away from each other. Do you hear me? Do not go near each other. I will try to come up with a viable solution."

Both replied, "Yes, Pastor…we hear you."

For the next three months, Pastor Tune separately counseled Mrs. Campbell and Bubba Casey on a weekly basis. Some progress was made, but Bubba began to withdraw…since some of his duties and responsibilities had been curtailed, especially in dealing and counseling with women.

As time went on, Bubba began to make little critical remarks toward the Pastor to some of his close friends. He would say things like, "If I were the Senior Pastor, I'd be more in tune with the people. I'd preach shorter sermons on Sunday mornings. If I were the Senior Pastor, I'd be more understanding and sympathetic to the people's needs. I'd be more sensitive. I'd be more tolerant…"

This type of faultfinding and criticism eventually expanded over to members, visitors and just about anyone who would listen.

On the outside, Bubba seemed confident, compassionate, good-natured, caring, and genuinely interested in the parishioners; nevertheless, on the inside he was developing into a carnivorous and ravenous wolf in sheep's clothing. He was angry and defiant. His insides were poison.

Remember Elders Joseph Pine and Timothy Little...the little evil people? Word about Bubba's discontent reached them one day when they were on the golf course. "Tim, we need to look into this. You know, Bubba is one of ours...one of the good old boys. If he is upset about something, then it's our job to rectify the situation. Bubba is like a brother. You know what I mean, don't you, Tim?" asked Pine.

"Yes, I believe I do, Joe. I'll look into it the first thing next week", replied Tim.

On Monday morning, Elder Tim Little, while driving his Mustang convertible, picked up his cell phone and called Bubba. "Bubba, this is Elder Tim Little. How you doing, old boy? What's going on with you?"

"Just fine and you?"

"Oh, I'm doing just great. Life is good. Listen, meet me at Martha's Diner for lunch...say, around noon. We need to talk, good buddy. OK?"

"Sure, I think that would be great. I'll see you then."

Little and Bubba arrived about the same time. Martha's Diner was packed as usual. People drove for miles around just to partake of the good old southern fried cuisine. Her food was fattening, yet so good and mouth-watering...And her homemade pies were sinful...simply sinful.

After sitting down, exchanging niceties, and ordering their Bar-B-Q ribs, Little said, "Ok, boy, let's talk. What's going on with you and Pastor Tune?"

Bubba began a string of lies and delivered an Oscar performance. He began, "Well, first of all...you must promise me confidentiality and anonymity. Do you get my drift?"

"Sure, you know me. I'm trustworthy. I'm as good as gold. My word is my bond. Remember, Bubba, we are of the same mold and fiber. You are one of us."

"OK, here's the scoop. Several months ago I caught our beloved Pastor Johnny Tune in a rather compromising situation...a sexual encounter with someone in the church. I will not divulge her identity because of my professionalism, honesty, and integrity. Because she came to me for counseling, I'm sworn to secrecy to protect her and to protect the church from a scandal. Of course, Pastor Tune has threatened me with expulsion and ostracism if I come forward. Do you see what I've been carrying around with me for the past few months? I have been a prisoner in my own church."

"Yes, the whole thing seems clear to me now. This would explain the rift between you two. Bubba, you did the right thing by confiding in me. I know this congregation. I'll call an emergency board meeting immediately. We'll take care of this matter."

"Elder Tim, I'd appreciate it if you would keep me out of this as much as possible. I do not want the people to think I'm a traitor or Judas...or that I would betray my longtime and faithful friend."

"You don't worry about a thing. That rascal will pay for this. In Waterford, we don't take too kindly to adultery. I just do not understand why Pastor Johnny would prostitute himself in this way. We pay that man well. We have taken good care of him, his wife, and family...now this. I guess lust finally overcame him. You go home and get some rest and stop worrying. The Church Board will deal with this affair. That's our job."

The next evening, Elder Little opened the meeting by saying, "Gentlemen, we are here tonight to discuss the agenda that was sent to you earlier. We need to reach a solution to our dilemma and predicament. It seems that we have ourselves in a pickle. What do we do? We are a church...a well-respected church. We have good people in this town. The floor is open for discussion and ideas. Who is first?"

"I move that we hang the Pastor by his toes," cried out one upset deacon.

"No, let's just kick him out gently," said another.

"I think we should hang him from the highest tree," someone suggested.

"I believe we should all reach a consensus tonight and then confront him," stated one of the elders.

"Of course, we're going to confront him. What the heck do you think we are going to do? But first, let's figure out what we are going to do with him," someone else said.

After about an hour, they came up with a brilliant plan, they thought.

"OK…Does everyone agree now that we will meet with Pastor Tune on Sunday evening after church and give him our decision? Do you all agree that we will ask for his resignation at that time? Furthermore, let it be stated in the record that he has been an outstanding pastor up until now; however, under the extenuating circumstances, we must ask for his resignation. Gentlemen, are we all in agreement?" asked Elder Joseph Pine.

"Yes," came the unanimous reply.

"Then it's a done deal and we will save the church from some embarrassing and unpleasant questions," said Elder Little.

Sunday evening came. Pastor Tune preached his last sermon on Blue Street that night. The title of his sermon was "True Friends of Integrity". Quite ironic, wouldn't you say?

After his sermon, the Church Board asked him to resign. Eventually, Pastor Johnny and Tamie Tune moved on to bigger and better things. They moved to Atlanta to accept a pastorate in a larger church with a much higher salary. In time, Pastor Tune forgave the elders, deacons, and Bubba Casey.

Years later…Pastor Tune was quoted as saying, "I met my Judas and I am still alive. Judas made me a better man. For this I am very thankful indeed!"

Chapter 9
THE VOYEUR

The whole town was going bananas. Reports of a "peeping tom" were rampant and intense. The Police Chief, Randolph Sweeney, had tried to calm the communities of Waterford by going on the local radio and TV stations with updated status reports.

"We're doing everything within our power to bring this individual to justice. Currently, we have several good leads. We expect to make an arrest within a few days," the Chief responded.

Within the past ten days the Waterford "peeping tom" had been seen by thirteen different women including three young teenagers. People were on edge.

One beautiful young lady with long brunette hair responded, "I was getting out of the shower, drying off, putting my panties on when I heard a noise just outside my window. As I looked up, I saw a man with a stocking over his head with a jogging suit on. He was in no hurry. He watched me pick up the phone and dial 911. He literally just stood there looking, smiling, and licking his lips. As I continued talking to the 911 operator, he eventually departed…What a fruitcake!"

Another attractive woman said, "I thought he was a burglar coming through the window to rob or rape me. However, he only stood there by the window looking at me in the nude. He had some sort of stupid looking stocking over his head. What a total @#$%^!"

Chief Sweeney hired extra off-duty policemen from surrounding areas to assist during this time of anxiety and apprehension…in this little harmonious and peaceful southern town.

The alert was on. Men were buying additional ammunition and some were even purchasing new handguns. The women were using extra precautions in their homes. Shades were drawn. Doors were double locked. Dogs were placed outside homes in strategic locations.

People were asked to jog only in pairs or in groups…and to be alert for anything out of the ordinary. In a word, this sleepy little village was reacting in an irritable and angry fashion. And who could blame them?

Someone asked, "How could anyone do this to our quiet and peaceful community? Whoever this is…has got to be a sick and confused individual. But we will survive. We always have. We will get this freak and pervert. Just wait and see."

***

One night after church basketball practice…at the gym located at The First Church on Blue Street…Deacon Atwater noticed that one of the players had slipped out the side door of the gym. He didn't think too much about it until the next morning. He picked up the morning paper and to his amazement…

There it was. The headlines read, "Peeping tom strikes again, this time on Blue Street."

The culprit had been spotted only two houses down from the church. This was within minutes of the time that Atwater had seen one of the players go out the side door of the gym. Who could this be? Was it someone on the church basketball team?

Deacon Atwater began to search his mind. "Let's see. On my team are Tim, Ted, Jim, Sam, and Charlie. On Elder Joseph Pine's team are Jack, Tod, Mike, Henry, and Matt. No…None of these could be the 'peeping tom'. I know these guys. They are all good, moral decent men. I must really be getting senile to think such a thing."

Suddenly, it dawned on Atwater who the perpetrator was.

"What a stupid jack and dunce I've been. It was there in front of me all the time. How could I have been such a fool? How could I have overlooked it? We have been playing basketball now for several long weeks…and we have been playing with a voyeur all this time. He needs help and fast. What can I do?" asked Atwater.

"No one will ever believe me. I must go secretly to Chief Sweeney. He'll know what to do."

Atwater called the Chief and said, "Chief, this is Chuck Atwater. We need to talk…quickly. I know who the peeping tom is. He is a mutual friend of ours. He is sick and needs help."

Chief Sweeney replied, "OK, meet me at Martha's Diner in half an hour."

Over a cup of hot coffee, the two began exchanging vital information. Soon, it was very evident that the voyeur was, in fact, a mutual friend.

"But how will we prove it?" asked Deacon Atwater.

The Chief replied, "I've got a plan. Shhhhh, listen to me..."

Friday night was going to be an important basketball match between The First Church and Zion Methodist. The "plan" was set in motion.

A lot of excitement was in the air. Much publicity had been generated and announced over the local radio stations. The two churches would share in the net proceeds (revenue) from the game's concessions and ticket sales. Three police agencies had been briefed on the plan and were indeed ready to stop this menace of the Waterford community.

Immediately after the game, one of the Blue Street players disappeared. When a count was taken of the players, sure enough, the Chief and Atwater were correct in their assumption...Their own mutual friend was missing...

The police went into action. Within thirty minutes, they had their suspect in custody. He had been caught five blocks away on Roosevelt Boulevard at Mayor Ned Coon's residence. The Mayor's wife, Laura, had been doing a little entertaining of her own. It seems that she and her lover, Billy Bob, had the bedroom all to themselves...or least they thought so...until the peeping tom was nabbed just outside the bedroom window.

Chief Sweeney briefed the mayor on the arrest, but did not mention the part about his wife's entertainment for the evening. The Chief felt that Mayor Coon already had too many issues and city concerns to deal with…at the moment. The peeping tom was captured. This was the good news.

The next morning, the front page of the Waterford Chronicle read, "One of our most prominent citizens has been arrested for the recent peeping tom activities in our community. Apparently, several months ago, the perpetrator had a complete nervous breakdown that left him with severe mental problems and a sexual disorder. In addition, it appears that the subject was wearing women's underclothes at the time of his arrest."

To the right of the article was a large photo of the alleged perpetrator. As you might have guessed, it was none other than our beloved Elder Joseph Pine…

Chapter 10
THE FUNERAL

Snow was on the ground. Seventy Five friends and family members had come to the cemetery to pay their last respects to Deacon Danny Frye. He had been a deacon for the last ten years at The First Church on Blue Street. He was a man of integrity, fairness, and responsibility. He loved his wife, family, friends, and his church. Now, some of the attendees were reminiscing.

Danny, age 48, had died of lung cancer. Some believed it was from smoking two packs of cigarettes a day. Danny always said, "Well, everybody's going to die of something someday...sometime." He refused to quit smoking. He died within a few short months.

After the doctors gave their prognosis and overall predictions, Danny laughed in their faces. "I will beat this like I have beaten other things in my life. As you know, I do not have an enemy in the whole world. After all, everyone loves me. I will not die, but I will live."

But now he was dead. Diane Frye would certainly miss her faithful husband passionately. Her eyes were still swollen from her tears. She asked herself, "How could this happen? Why, God, did you take Danny? He was a good man. You know everyone loved him and he loved them. Why did this happen?"

Several days earlier, Diane had been comforted by Elder Luke Cole. During the funeral arrangements, Luke assisted her with many of the burial details. It was the least he could do for the Frye family.

The night before the funeral, Luke visited the Frye family home...alone. The only person present was Diane; therefore, he went in to see if any other details needed his attention.

"Come on in, Luke. I certainly do appreciate all that you and The First Church have done for me during this terrible ordeal. I couldn't have made it without you, Luke. Come here and give me a great big hug," she loudly suggested.

That big hug turned into several hugs and kisses that evening...and eventually into several hours of bedtime sex. At 1:00 AM, Luke said, "Look Diane, I really must be going. Now, don't you feel bad or guilty about what happened here tonight, you hear? After all, I'm sure Danny would have wanted you to be happy and taken care of...in every way. You know he wants you to be happy, don't you?"

"Yes, I do. I'll see you at the funeral, Luke. Don't you feel guilty either," responded Diane.

Luke quickly drove home and slowly inched his way up the driveway with his car lights off. He sneaked into the living room and slept on the couch that night.

***

The next day, the ground was covered with snow, but the sun came out and the funeral went rather well. The family seemed to be in good spirits. They had indeed lost a good man. Diane and

Luke made eye contact at least a dozen times at the funeral and graveside ceremony...

Several weeks passed. Elder Luke Cole had to be out of town on business for several days. When he returned, he had received a message to call Mrs. Frye. She wanted some advice.

Luke called her and made an appointment to see her. He told his wife, Esther, that he was assisting Diane with her insurance affairs and burial benefits...and not to wait up for him.

He arrived about 8 PM. This time...he didn't leave until 3 AM. As he was putting his pants and shirt back on and preparing to leave, Diane whispered, "Luke, I need to tell you something, but I don't know how. I've been waiting for the right moment."

Luke replied, "Diane, you are so sweet; however, Sweetheart, I really must go. What is it you want to tell me?"

Diane looked at Luke...took him by the hand and said, "Luke, I'm pregnant with your child..."

Chapter 11
THE MOST EXTREME DESPERATE HOUSEWIFE in WATERFORD

Things for Margie Smith were tough because she was indeed a lonely housewife who definitely wanted to be loved and appreciated by her husband Danny Joe. For the past six years, Danny had been very distant with Margie. One day Margie asked, "What the heck is wrong with you. Why do you ignore me, refuse to talk to me, refuse to have sex with me...sometimes for weeks? Tell me, I need to know."

Danny responded, "Margie, I must confess to you. I am addicted to porn. I have been lying to you for several years now. Every chance I get, I watch porn...sometimes late at night on TV or on our computer...and other times when I go on business trips. Sometimes I even visit strip joints. I have tried to quit, but I am a porn addict. I have talked to the new pastor (Jim Dean) on Blue Street, but it has not helped me. Don't you think I would quit if I could?"

Margie: "I am telling you right now, Danny. You are ruining our marriage. Perhaps, if we both went in together for counseling, that would help."

Danny: "Well, it might. I will talk with Pastor Dean this Sunday."

Each day it got harder for Margie to understand the rationale behind Danny's love for porn. She felt bad. She felt sad. She even blamed herself for his sin, but deep down, she knew that he would have to take a stand himself in order to overcome this addition.

Months later, they were still being counseled by Pastor Jim Dean. Not much was being accomplished according to Margie. Danny was still distant and un-attentive to her needs. In Margie's eyes, Danny was guilty of infidelity and she was hurting deep inside. The pain was growing.

Three months went by ever so slowly; however, one day, Margie had a water pipe to burst in the main bathroom. She called Pipe's Plumbing immediately. Guess what? Yeah! A strong handsome plumber (Greg) showed up about 30 minutes later to fix the pipe. He knocked on the door and Margie invited him in. She noticed that he was tall, dark, and handsome...had a great big smile and a cute rear-end.

Greg went into the bathroom and surveyed the damage. He looked at her and said, "We'll have this fixed in no time at all."

Meantime, Margie made some fresh, ice-cold, sweet tea with lemon and offered Greg a glass. He accepted. They sat down on the sofa near the master bedroom and made small talk...all the while observing each other and wondering how each would be in bed.

Margie later explained it this way, "Our eyes met. Our eyes lingered a little too long. He touched my hand. My heart began to pound louder and louder. We kissed. We fooled around. We made love. After all, my marriage was falling apart anyway. I had not felt like a woman in years. It seemed like…Greg and I were just meant to be with one another. At that point, I knew that Danny and I were finished as man and wife. I had no love or passion for him any longer. We were through."

***

Months passed. Margie continued to explain her actions in her own mind, "Even though I knew this affair was wrong, I became addicted in the same way that my ex-husband was addicted to porn. I allowed things to happen that should not have happened. My mind was in a tailspin. I didn't know what to do. Greg was also a married man. He had been separated from his wife for several months. He told me that he loved me. In my head, I believed him, but in my heart I did not."

Margie continued to see Greg for about a year. She soon learned that she would have to deal with all of her pent-up anger toward her ex-husband…Danny in a more positive way. She wanted to get past the hurt and move forward. Was this possible?

Margie also continued her weekly therapy with Pastor Dean. One day, she said, "Pastor Dean, I have a problem. I blame myself for a lot of my past disappointments. Sometimes, I feel like a fool. My marriage was a failure. My life has been a failure. I believe the problems were mostly my fault. Sometimes, I feel like a whore. You know my faith was strong at one time…prior to all of this happening to me. I have been shaken to the core. I know that God ordained marriage, but I had to take a stand and move on. Do you understand what I am saying?"

Pastor Dean: Margie, a small portion of this was your fault, but most of it was not. Your spouse let you down. You tried to iron it out, but it just couldn't be done. Too much water had gone under the bridge. The milk had been spilled. The egg had been broken and you could not put it back together again. You still have faith. You are still God's child. This too will pass, my Dear.

Margie: Does this mean that I will always be branded as an adulteress? Does this mean that I will go to hell?

Pastor Dean: No, God forgives. We all make mistakes. None of us is perfect. That is why we need to go to church, pray, and talk to God about these things.

Margie: You are right Pastor. I need to get back in church again. I have already broken off my relationship with Greg. It was extremely difficult. Even now, there are times when I want to call him and arrange a rendezvous, but I know that is not the long-term answer. I refuse to play any more games with Greg or with others.

Pastor Dean: Margie, I know you have been hurt very badly. It probably feels like Danny ripped your heart out...and I am sure he did. However, you must also forgive yourself for the long-term affair you had with Greg. Yes, you were infatuated with Greg. But now, you have come clean with yourself and with God. I believe you will truly find peace and feel better about yourself as you journey on the road to recovery. Why? Because you now have hope!

Margie: Hope? Thank you Pastor Dean. I needed to hear that.

Chapter 12
THE LOVE TRIANGLE

Let's take a look at the scenario: Deacon Howard T. Grant has been called a woman's man, a womanizer, one handsome dude, meticulous, a man with a great physique, a man who has a passion for women, gigolo, an authority on travel and good wine, and an exercise freak. He has been divorced three times so far. Lonely women flock to his door for love and companionship. He is not a bad person...just a lonely, hurt, dissatisfied, and shallow person. Deacon Grant is now in his early 50s. His hair is graying around his temples, but he is still a good-looking guy who looks ten years younger than his true age.

Now enters a previous high school and college queen and debutante...Ms. Silvia Lopez. Silvia (a divorcee, 42 years of age) falls in love with the gigolo...Deacon Grant. He tells her how beautiful she is...how he can't live without her...how she is the new woman in his life. They date. They dine together frequently. They drink wine together. They make love. They travel together to exotic places. Silvia is having the time of her life. She feels fulfilled and satisfied as a woman. Everything is coming up peaches and cream for her...Until...

Jessica Brown shows up. Jess as most people call her...is a widow on the prowl. She was married to Bob Brown for 25 wonderful years; however, he died two years ago and now, she wants to find another man who will love her passionately like her previous husband. Therefore, she is open to dating again...providing the man is handsome, passionate, good looking, and generous. She has her eyes on Deacon Howard T. Grant. Who else?

One Sunday morning after church, they see each other at the fellowship center downstairs. At first, they engage in small talk. How's the weather? How are you doing? What's happening in your life, etc.? Then Deacon Grant asked Jessica for a date... dinner at Outback's on Tuesday night. She accepted. He was delighted.

On Tuesday night, Deacon Grant arrives precisely on time. They say their "greetings" and off they go. On the way to Outback's, he tells her how beautiful she is...how he had admired her for several months...hoping they would meet formally at some point.

She said, "I have admired and wanted you for over a year. You seem to be the nicest and sexiest man in the church right now. You have a great body. You know how to talk to people, especially women. You know a lot about travel and great wines."

Grant replies, "Well, thank you for those kind remarks. I have to admit...I do love women. Women are special, lovely, enjoyable, curvy, and incredible beautiful creations."

Jess: Tell me something Howard. What do you think of me so far? Am I attractive? Am I the type of woman you enjoy being around? Am I sexy?

Grant: Jess, you are the epitome of Eve, the woman that had everything...sexy, voluptuous, sensual, and so desirable. You remind me so much of the woman in the Garden of Eden...innocence.

Jess: So, you do think I am sexy and passionate?

Grant: Absolutely! You are the type of woman that every man wants to sleep with…no exceptions.

Jess: Okay then…let's get some food and see where this goes.

They arrive at Outback's and go in to be seated. They order a couple of draft beers and an appetizer (Bloomin' Onion)…and then wait for the waiter to receive their orders. They chit chat and have a bunch of small talk, but then get serious about the evening.

Grant: If it's okay with you, after dinner, we will go to my house for a nightcap…so that we can get to know each other better. Is that oaky with you, Jess?

Jess: Certainly…I think it's a great idea. Let's do it.

After two New York strips, salad, baked potato, appetizer, and two beers, they leave the restaurant for Grant's home. They arrive moments later.

Jess: This is such a beautiful home. How do you keep it so nice, neat, and clean?

Grant: I have a maid that comes in twice a week…and sometimes, I vacuum and tidy up a bit myself.

Jess: Super…I like a man who is tidy and clean.

Grant: Jess, would you like a gin and tonic?

Jess: Yes, I would. Thanks.

Grant: Here you are Love. I hope you enjoy it.

Jess: Thanks. What is that music I hear?

Grant: It's music from the 60s and 70s. Do you like it?

Jess: Certainly…It's wonderful. It makes me feel sexy and wild.

Grant: You know, I think I am falling in love with you. You are such an incredible and desirable woman. You are so sexy…well built…and beautiful. What am I to do?

Jess: I think you should make love to me right now. I have not been with a man since my husband died two years ago. Do you think you can handle me?

Grant: Darling, if I can't handle you, nobody can. Let's go to my bedroom.

They go to the master bedroom…and make wild, passionate love for the next four hours. They moan, groan, scream, and make passionate noises. Eventually, the night is over. Grant takes Jess home…says goodbye…and makes another date with her… Friday night.

Meantime, Deacon Grant gets a phone call from…you know who…Silvia Lopez.

Silvia: Hey Howard, it's me. I tried to reach you last night, but there was no answer. Where were you?

Howard: Right…my phone was acting up. I think it was off the hook or something. Darling, what do you need? Is there something that I can help you with?

Silvia: No, I just wanted to talk to you…to see what you were doing…that sort of thing.

Howard: I'm fine. Hey, let's get together Thursday night…if that's okay.

Silvia: That sounds great. Pick me up around 6:30 PM. Is that okay with you?

Howard: Absolutely. That's perfect. You are such a sweet-heart. I love you.

Silvia: I love you too…See you Thursday night.

***

Meantime, back to reality…Jess calls and talks to Howard several times during the day. They talk about love, sex, and the future. Jess has no clue about the other woman…Silvia. Jess thinks that she is the only woman for Howard…the only one that can satisfy him sexually and socially.

Two months later, Howard is still keeping up this charade. Because of all the activity in which he is engaged, he looks tired, worn out, depleted, and exhausted. He doesn't know which end is up. He is now falling asleep in church. He is late for appointments. He looks like he needs a long vacation and an oxygen mask. And then suddenly, it happens…

The two sexy women accidently meet at Martha's Diner for breakfast at the same time one morning. Jess sees Silvia and invites her over to her table.

Jess: I see you all the time at church. How are you doing these days, Silvia?

Silvia: I am doing fine honey. How about you?

Jess: Just great…I have found the most wonderful and caring man. He is such a delight to be around.

Silvia: Wonderful…Who is this incredible man?

Jess: I hesitate to tell you because you might be jealous. We go to dinners, plays, out of town resorts, and we serve on the same board at the First Church on Blue Street. He is such a generous and kind man. I am so happy.

Silvia: This is wonderful. Who is this mystery man? Do I know him?

Jess: You may have seen him, but I don't think you know him. I really don't think he is your type.

Silvia: Okay, tell me. The suspense is killing me.

Jess: All right then, but you must promise not to tell this news all over the church. Do I have your word on this?

Silvia: Absolutely, you can trust me. "Mum's" the word.

Jess: Okay. Here goes. His name is Deacon Howard T. Grant. He is such a wonderful man of integrity, honor, and family values. Do you know him?

Silvia: You little slut. Howard and I have been going together for the past three years. What the !@#$%^ are you doing with my man? He loves me. I love him. We travel. We go to bed together. We are true friends. We are soul mates. What the !@@#$%^ are you doing pussyfooting around with my man? Are you nuts? I ought to pull all of your hair out and claw your eyes out. What is wrong with you?

Jess: I am so sorry. I didn't know. He said he was single and not involved with anyone. Silvia, I want to apologize. This is not something that I would do deliberately...if I had known. How can I make this up to you?

Silvia: Never mind...I can see that you truly are innocent and did not know about us. In this case, he is the jackass...the weasel. Let's give him a taste of his own medicine, shall we?

Jess: What do you have in mind? What can I do?

Silvia discussed her plan with Jess and they decided that her plan was the best course of action. They set it in motion.

***

One week later, the plan unfolded: Silvia had made a date with Howard for Saturday evening. They drive to Outback's.

Howard and Silvia arrived about 6:30 PM…had cocktails… and then ordered their steaks. As their steaks arrived at their table, so did Jess.

Jess: Howard, what the !@#$%^ are doing here with this woman? I thought you and I were in love. I thought I was your special soul mate. I thought we had a future together.

Howard: Who are you? Do I know you? Silvia, do you know this woman?

Silvia: Yes, I do. I know that you have been going to bed with her, making love to her, and traveling with her to exotic places. What do you have to say about this?

Howard: I don't know what you are talking about. I have never seen this woman before in my life.

Jess: What a liar you are. We have served on numerous boards together at church. We have traveled together for the past two months…to several vacation hot spots…Made love continuously…ate in the finest restaurants. Are you saying you don't know me? Are you nuts?

Howard: Okay, look…Yes, I believe it's coming back to me now…Yes, I think I remember. But Jess, you mean nothing to me. You were there as a substitute…never the real thing.

Silvia: Howard, it's over. Never call me again. Never speak to me again. Never write me another email. Never think about me again! Goodbye.

Jess: Howard you can go to !@#$%^&. You and I are though. You are a sick puppy. You need help. I should kick you in the testicles, but I'm a lady. Good-bye.

Howard sat alone for a long time just thinking. He had screwed up and he knew it. Read on…

That Sunday, shameless Howard met another divorced, sexy, beautiful woman who did not know him. They had their first date the following Friday night…and the beat goes on.

Chapter 13
WHO KILLED JACK HENRY?

Waterford was a growing town. Most visitors loved Waterford. It was a beautiful place to live. People were moving to Waterford because it was such a peaceful little town...most of the time. It was a wonderful, quiet community for raising and rearing children.

However, one tragic late afternoon, Jack Henry, a deacon at Blue Street, was murdered...shot to death in his own home. He loved animals. He loved the big outdoors. He loved hunting and fishing. Although he loved his family, his biggest passion was horses.

Remember Mrs. Jill St Cloud? Her sister discovered that Jill also had an interest in horses. Jill would go out several times a week to the Waterford Stables. She was supposed to be riding horses; however, she was not riding horses, but riding Jack Henry, the deacon.

Jill also loved the outdoors and she occasionally rode horses...Her biggest fan and lover was Jack.

Even though Jill was married to another man, she looked up to Jack as her protector.

For five years, Jack and Jill had an illicit love affair going on. They spent every spare moment together, mostly at the Waterford Stables. But neither of them could have known what was going to happen on May 1st of that year.

Jill remembers the last time she saw Jack. It was a sunny spring day...not a cloud in the sky. "He told me he loved me and then kissed me goodbye."

Late that afternoon, Jack left the stables and headed home. As he arrived home, he noticed that the garage door was open... something he considered odd. The door was always closed except for leaving or entering the garage.

He parked his car in the garage and went inside. When he stepped inside the kitchen, someone fired a gun. He was hit three times in the heart area. As he lay motionless on the blood-stained floor, the intruder departed. His wife Susan was in the master bedroom at the time. She heard the shots and ran out to see what had happened. She immediately called 911. She was worried that someone might still be in the home; so, she began to search the house, but found nothing. The killer or killers had departed.

Waterford detectives found very few clues at the crime scene. They said that Jack had been murdered by someone who was very angry...perhaps even execution-style...three gun shot wounds to the heart. There were no eyewitnesses...no murder weapon...no fingerprints...very little to go on.

One of the investigators, Detective Scott Moore, said, "This does not look right. I think it might have been staged as a burglary to cover up the murder. I think his killer knew him and wanted him dead."

The house appeared to have been burglarized, but valuable jewelry and other expensive items were not taken. The only physical evidence at the crime scene was found on Jack's body. His shirt had three bullet holes at close range. No bullet casings were found.

One of the few leads early in the case came from Jack himself. According to Jill, several hours before he was murdered, Jack had received a troubling and disconcerting phone call. He told Jill that it was nothing...just someone who was upset about something. Even though Jack looked concerned, he did not seem to take it seriously.

Elder Luke Cole from Blue Street spoke to one of the detectives and said, "You don't know Jack, do you? You really do not know Jack. Jack was a peculiar person. I know him quite well. As a matter of fact, I have known him since childhood. He was sneaky, unscrupulous, devious, unprincipled, and dishonest. How he became a deacon at the First Church on Blue Street is a mystery to me.

So the question continues: Who killed Jack Henry and why?

***

Well, it seems that Deacon Jack had disappointed several people from the First Church on Blue Street, especially in his business dealings. He was a real estate broker and owned Henry's Real Estate Company. A large number of his clients attended First Church on Blue Street. Over the years, Jack or some of his agents had managed to make a few unscrupulous and dishonest blunders in some of their real estate deals.

For example, Mrs. Eva Johnson...a long time resident and wealthy widow of Waterford had bought some prime property... about 40 acres on the outskirts of town. Jack Henry was her broker in the negotiations. It seems that Mr. Henry had told Mrs. Johnson that the land had been zoned and approved for residential housing development. The lots needed to be a minimum of a half-acre. However, upon the completion of the deal, Eva Johnson found out later that the land had yet to be zoned and approved for residential development. The land had not met the "perk test" which meant that the land was not suitable for drainage of septic systems. The contract did not read, "Land to perk to customer's satisfaction." The lack of this little phrase cost Mrs. Johnson over a million dollars. The Waterford Zoning Commission and Health Department told her that the property would probably never perk.

The Johnson case was not an isolated incident. Over the years, there had been many deceitful and questionable real estate ventures. After Jack Henry closed a deal, he was nowhere to found if anything went wrong after a closing. He would not answer phone calls, emails, or letters if it looked like a potential problem was developing. This type of business behavior did not make him any friends and eventually cost him a lot of "repeat" business.

As a matter of fact, Deacon Jack Henry had recently filed Chapter 11 Bankruptcy on behalf of his company.

Now, let's get back to the question. Who killed Deacon Jack and why? Was it his lover's husband? Was it a business client who had received a raw deal from Jack? Was it a business associate who had a beef with Jack Henry? Was it Jack's wife? Was it his lover Jill St Cloud? Was it a Blue Street parishioner? Who was it? Who was angry at Jack so much that he/she wanted Jack dead?

We know it was not the butler, the cook, or the baker because Jack had none of these in his employment.

A few days after the funeral of Jack Henry, Detective Scott Moore came across some very interesting information that could be damaging to Mrs. Susan Henry. It seems that she had recently taken out an additional insurance policy on Jack for the amount of one million dollars. Detective Moore certainly had some questions to ask her.

The next day at the Waterford Police Department, Susan Henry was interrogated and interviewed by Detective Moore. This is what went down:

Moore: Mrs. Henry, is it true that you recently took out a million dollar insurance policy on Mr. Henry?

Susan: Yes, but I didn't kill him. With our real estate company going down hill, I needed some additional financial security.

Moore: Let's go back over the moments right before Jack was killed. Where were you in the house?

Susan: I was in the hallway when I heard the shots.

Moore: You were in the hallway? On the day of his murder, you said that you were in your bedroom.

Susan: Well…I…was sort of…I was in…the hallway in front of my bedroom.

Moore: Now, let me get this straight. You were near your bedroom in the hallway. Is this correct?

Susan: Yes, that is right.

Moore: Okay…Your husband arrives. He parks his car in the garage. Did you hear the garage door open?

Susan: Yes, I did.

Moore: That's strange because one of your neighbors stated that the garage door was open for at least two hours prior to the shots being fired.

Susan: Well…Well…I…was shook up after hearing the shots and seeing my husband lying on the floor. Maybe I was mistaken. Maybe I didn't hear the garage door open. I'm not sure.

Moore: Mrs. Henry, is your home equipped with an alarm system?

Susan: Yes.

Moore: Did you have the alarm set that day?

Susan: Yes, we always have our alarm system activated when we are inside the house.

Moore: Did the alarm go off that day prior to the shooting?

Susan: No, I would have heard it, I'm sure.

Moore: Mrs. Susan Henry, I think you are lying. You have admitted that your alarm system was always activated when you were at home and not in the yard. Tell me, who put the garage door up that day?

Susan: Well, I must have. I was out in the lawn that afternoon for a while. It must have been me. I just don't remember.

Moore: Listen, I have just been told that I have an urgent phone call in the main office. I will be right back. Please help yourself to some coffee or a Coke.

Detective Scott Moore went down the hallway to answer the phone.

Moore picked up the receiver and said, "Hello. How can I help you?"

"This is Sheriff Larry Joe Franks. Detective Moore, I have some great news for you. I have solved the murder case of Jack Henry."

Moore: What do you mean? I have a prime suspect in my interrogation room right now.

Franks: Listen to me. A certain Mrs. Eva Johnson came in today and confessed to Jack's murder.

Moore: What are you talking about. I'm telling you, I have his killer in the interrogation room right now. Mrs. Johnson could not be the perpetrator.

Franks: Detective Moore, you have the wrong person.

Moore: What do you mean...I have the wrong person?

Franks: It seems that Mrs. Eva Johnson was deceived and manipulated by our friend Jack...several months ago in regards to a land deal that went bad. She thought that she was purchasing some prime property near Waterford, but it turned out to be a white elephant. She lost a bundle...about a million dollars. She wanted revenge. She waited patiently for months. Finally, she saw her opportunity. She had staked out the home of Jack Henry several times in the past few days before the murder. On this particular day, the garage door was up, so she sneaked inside and hid in the kitchen pantry until Jack came home...and then boom. She killed him! Can you believe it?

Moore: Are you kidding me, Sheriff?

Franks: No, I have already booked her and locked her up in my jail. The DA's Office has filed murder charges against her.

Moore: Okay. Thanks. I still can't believe it. We will talk later.

At this point, Detective Moore went back to the interrogation room and released Mrs. Susan Henry. She left immediately.

Susan went directly to the local insurance agency in Waterford and asked them the status of the million-dollar insurance policy check. She wanted to know when she would have access to the funds. They told her that it would be about 72 hours after they received a certified copy of the death certificate.

Susan departed the insurance office and went straight to the county jail to visit Eva Johnson. Susan said to Eva, "Darling, it's done. The million dollars will be available within 72 hours after they receive the death certificate. I'm glad it's over. Baby, there is no way that you will be convicted. We have a million reasons that will point to a "not-guilty" plea. The defense attorney that I have hired says that he will get you off on a 'technicality'. He has not lost a case in five years. He knows every judge in this part of the state. We will get you out of here on bail tomorrow...and then we can continue our hot, sexy, passionate relationship. Is that a deal?"

Eva replies, "Absolutely, my Darling. Thanks for taking care of the bail. Today, we both win. You get rid of a lying scoundrel who was having one affair after another and I get sweet revenge on Jack Henry...who cheated me out of a million dollars. Not many people knew Jack...not really. He was some piece of work...a work of crapola...a worthless human being."

Now you and I can get on with our lives...live together in love and peace. Life is good, Baby. Life is good!"

Secret Last Words about Love

Believe it or not, almost every situation in this novel actually happened in real life in various towns and cities across America. Of course, the names and places have been changed to protect the guilty. Some of you may not think that this book is appropriate; however, some of you will watch the identical thing on TV, Utube, DVD, or at the movies and think nothing about it. Is this book appropriate for the times? I don't know. You be the judge. My intent in writing this book was not to focus on the problems or sins of our society and church, but to ask the question, "What is the solution to this type of behavior displayed by some of our outstanding citizens, community leaders, and church members?"

As much as MURDER is a staple in mystery stories, so is love. Love is a four-letter word, which represents the greatest of the trio of faith, hope, and love. It may appear in a mystery as the driving force behind the plot and the characters. Or it may appear as a sub-plot, a light spot in a heavy story. However, it is there. An emotion this strong gets a lot of attention. Love has its own special way.

How do we keep romance and love alive? Take the hand of your lover right now and look her directly in the eyes and say, "You are my best friend. You are my Sweetheart. I love you. I highly respect you. You belong to me. I belong to you. I love you so very much! You are valuable to me. I need you. I am yours. You are mine. I love you!"

Your Sweetheart (lover) is Your Best Friend.

***

As love partners, we must have clear channels of open communication. I'm not talking about computers/laptops/cell phones/faxes, etc. So, what am I saying? As a whole, men are not doing a very good job of communicating, especially in the bedroom. Self-disclosure and transparency may be an invitation to be vulnerable, but it helps you to see things, feel things, and hope for things that you never thought possible.

Think thoughts of love. Speak words of love. Demonstrate unconditional love through the things that you do! Openness means being willing to communicate your deepest feelings. There can be no intimacy without conversation. Truthful communication moves your love spouse and creates a condition of unity, love, and satisfaction.

LISTENING to your spouse is also important. We must listen (learn to listen) to one another.

GIVE ONE ANOTHER SPACE: Do not suffocate each other. Love is letting go when your partner needs a break…some space…and holding her close when she needs care.

Don't smother each other. No one can grow in the shade or under a tight basket.

The Secret: The lover lets the other lover be free. Everyone is different. Different spouses require different mixes of independence and mutuality. But with careful listening and communication, and discussion, you can reach a happy medium. Whatever you do, do NOT become overly possessive. "Love is not possessiveness".

This is quite ironic, but true: **The more possessive we are and the more love we demand, the less we receive.** While the more freedom we give and the less we demand, the more love we receive. Let each other be free...and alive!

You may be separate individuals, yet love makes you one... and if you are like most couples, you are still becoming one. You did not get married to become a whole person. You were a whole person before you married your life partner. Two whole people come together to complement the other and to make one. I call this a team effort...a partnership...a union...a family entity. Even though we contribute to our partner's happiness or sometimes unhappiness, no one can make you truly happy but you and God. You need to be secure before you get married. But many of us were not! It takes "time" to become secure within a husband/wife relationship.

DO NOT think for one moment that you are the only person who matters to your lover or partner. We all have in-laws/out-laws, friends, loved ones, and children. Be real. No one person can meet all of your needs. Your spouse/love partner is, and will always be #1 in your life, but not the only person in whom you interact.

I fully expect my wife to have other interests other than me. I must extend freedom to her in which to develop those interests in other people, hobbies, volunteer work, etc. This only empowers our relationship. Freedom can never confine. It can never be detrimental to the relationship. It can only open up many exciting and undiscovered opportunities to enjoy life. When my wife Karen is pursuing the areas in which she excels, she is happy. I enjoy her most when she is happy. People are easier to love when they are happy. "If Mama ain't happy, ain't nobody happy!"

The stronger and more secure we become, the more we are willing to be ourselves while encouraging our spouse/love partner to do the same. Genuine unconditional love not only respects the individuality of the other, but also actually seeks to cultivate it. The ultimate goal: Spiritual growth, individual growth, social growth, and family growth.

WEIGH YOUR WORDS: Someone once said, "You cannot un-ring a bell!"

Words are Powerful. They can bring forth a wound or a healing. A wise spouse/marriage partner is aware of the potential damage loose words can cause, especially words spoken in anger.

Sometimes, we speak what we feel without considering the consequences of the pain/conflict that the words might bring to our spouses.

Speaking out words will put in motion a law...the law of cause and effect. We (as husbands) need to speak words of encouragement, understanding, love, caring words, positive words, and productive words.

Marriage relationships DO NOT die by themselves. We can kill a marriage relationship by inappropriate words…words spoken from the head and not from the heart, especially in a fit of rage or moment of anger! Words once spoken cannot be recalled. Do not insist on giving the last word!

Let the past be the past. The past is gone forever. Do not keep bringing up the past. Rehearsing past failures is non-productive and very un-romantic! It simply does not work. In addition, if something does not work, we need to stop doing it. Focus on what you want in your relationship. Focus on the present and future…your goals, aspirations, and destiny. Never underestimate the power of words. They can wound or they can heal.

FORGIVENESS: Forgiveness is often misunderstood. We must forgive one another. If we do not, anger, resentment, and hostility will build up! "If we really want to love, we must learn how to forgive" (Mother Theresa). Forgiveness works! However, it is difficult at times, but it works. Sometimes, we have to go to the person who wronged us…and say, "OK, we need to talk." To not forgive someone is the same as taking poison.

Forgiveness is a gift that you give yourself. It is not something you do FOR someone else. It is not complicated. It is simple. Sometimes, it may be saying to yourself, "I forgive you. All is forgiven". Forgiveness is an act of love. It challenges you to give up destructive thoughts. It builds confidence that you can survive the pain and grow from it. Telling someone is a bonus. When you forgive, you do it for you, not necessarily for the other person. If you do not forgive the person, that person owns you. Remember: The choice to forgive is always yours. Do it for you.

Forgiveness is a Choice! You do not have to forgive, but there are dire consequences. Refusing to forgive by holding on to the anger, resentment and a sense of betrayal can make your own life miserable. A vindictive mind-set creates bitterness and lets the betrayer claim one more victim. There is nothing so bad that cannot be forgiven. Nothing!

Healing begins with forgiveness! Focus your energy on the healing, not the hurt! HEALTHY love relationships are not possible without forgiveness. You cannot have a loving and rewarding relationship with anyone else, much less yourself, if you continue to hold on to things that happened in the past.

Regardless of the situation, making peace with people, i.e., your parents, spouse, CHILDREN, your boss, or anyone…is the only way to have a "healthy" relationship with yourself and others! Forgiving someone else is to agree within yourself to overlook the wrong they have committed against you and to move on with your life.

Unforgiveness brings the by-products of…inner conflict, struggle, unrest, anxiety, and depression. Unforgiveness will also affect your self-esteem and self-confidence!

"FORGIVE and FORGET is a MYTH". You may never forget. The Bible tells us to forgive. It does not say that we will forget the wrong. Some will say that we must not only forgive, but we must also forget. This is a myth and is not supported by Scripture. Nowhere does the Bible say that we must forgive and forget. It simply says for us to forgive. Only God has the capacity to forgive and forget at the same time. We do not. Read on…

However, we do have a choice to forgive…**Forgiveness is a choice**. As life goes on and you remember the matter again, just remember that you have already forgiven. Mentally forgive again if necessary, and then move forward. Over time, the vividness of the memory and hurt will fade. As Romantics (in love with each other), together we remember. In addition, if we plan to stay together, we will forgive.

Forgiveness is a creative act that changes us from prisoners of the past to free people of the present. It is not forgetfulness, but it involves accepting the promise that the future can be more than dwelling on memories of past injury. There is no future in the past. You can never live in the present and create a new and exciting future for yourself and your love partner…if you always stay stuck in the past. You CAN let go…and forgive. It takes no strength to let go…only courage. It takes a lot of energy to hold on to unforgiveness. It takes less energy to create a new and exciting relationship TOGETHER…a relationship anchored in unconditional love.

Forgiveness is another key to our own happiness. Forgiving someone takes moral courage. Forgiveness means choosing to let go, move on, and favor the positive. Love is an act of forgiveness.

"To forgive is the highest and most beautiful form of love. In return, you will receive untold peace and happiness" (Robert Muller).

Furthermore, you and I both know that there is only One Eternal Solution to any problem or situation on Planet Earth… and His Name is Jesus Christ. AMEN!

www.ingramcontent.com/pod-product-compliance
Lightning Source LLC
Chambersburg PA
CBHW071136250626
47159CB00006B/2244